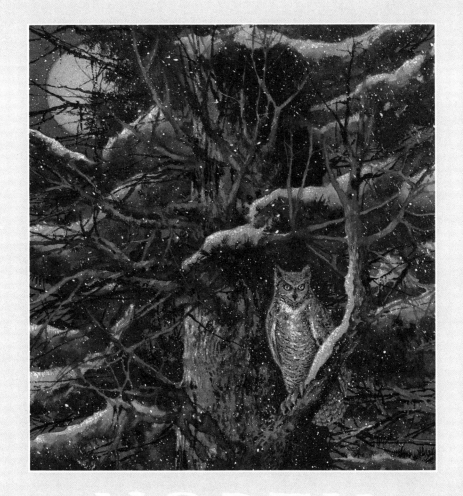

# NORTH
# COUNTRY
# NIGHT

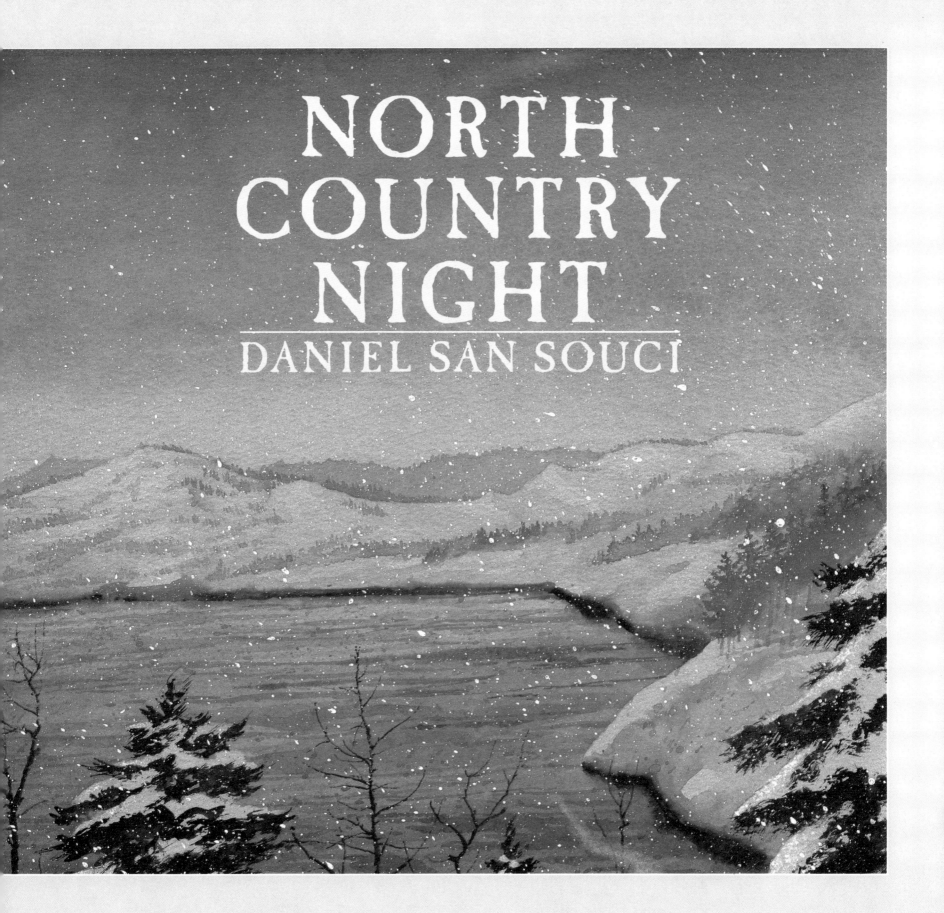

# NORTH
# COUNTRY
# NIGHT

## DANIEL SAN SOUCI

A PICTURE YEARLING BOOK

Grateful acknowledgment is given to the Lindsay Museum in Walnut Creek, California

Published by
Bantam Doubleday Dell Books for Young Readers
a division of
Bantam Doubleday Dell Publishing Group, Inc.
1540 Broadway
New York, New York 10036

The trademark Yearling® is registered in the U.S. Patent and Trademark Office.

The trademark Dell® is registered in the U.S. Patent and Trademark Office.

ISBN: 0-440-41029-0

Reprinted by arrangement with Doubleday Books for Young Readers

Printed in the United States of America

October 1994

10 9 8 7 6 5 4

UPR

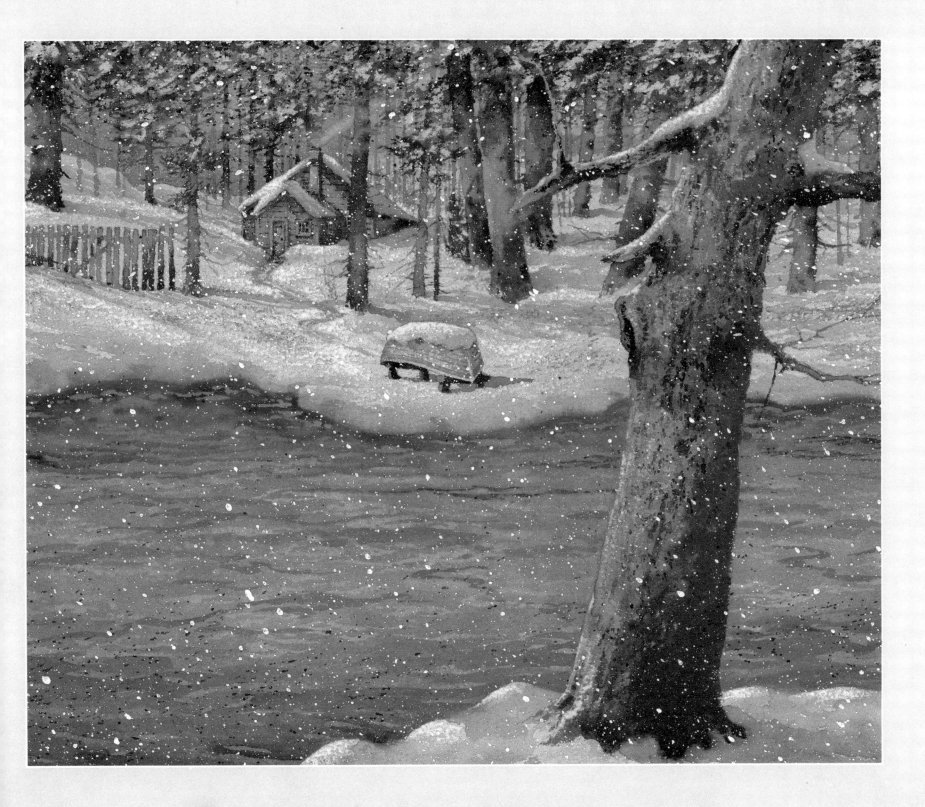

Snow is falling and it's nighttime in the North Country. One by one the lights go off in the cedar-sided cabin that overlooks the deep blue lake. Now it is time for the forest to come alive with the creatures of the night.

Under the winter moon the great horned owl glides over the roof of the cabin and circles above the tops of the giant pine trees. He is searching for prey with his keen yellow eyes.

Soon the owl locates movement in the cool shadows below the trees. A gray coyote lopes effortlessly through the fresh snow. Although the owl is a fierce predator, he will not disturb the coyote.

At the edge of the timber the coyote finds the tracks of a red fox. The coyote knows it would not be easy to catch the clever fox. But instinct tells him that the fox may have picked up the scent of food,

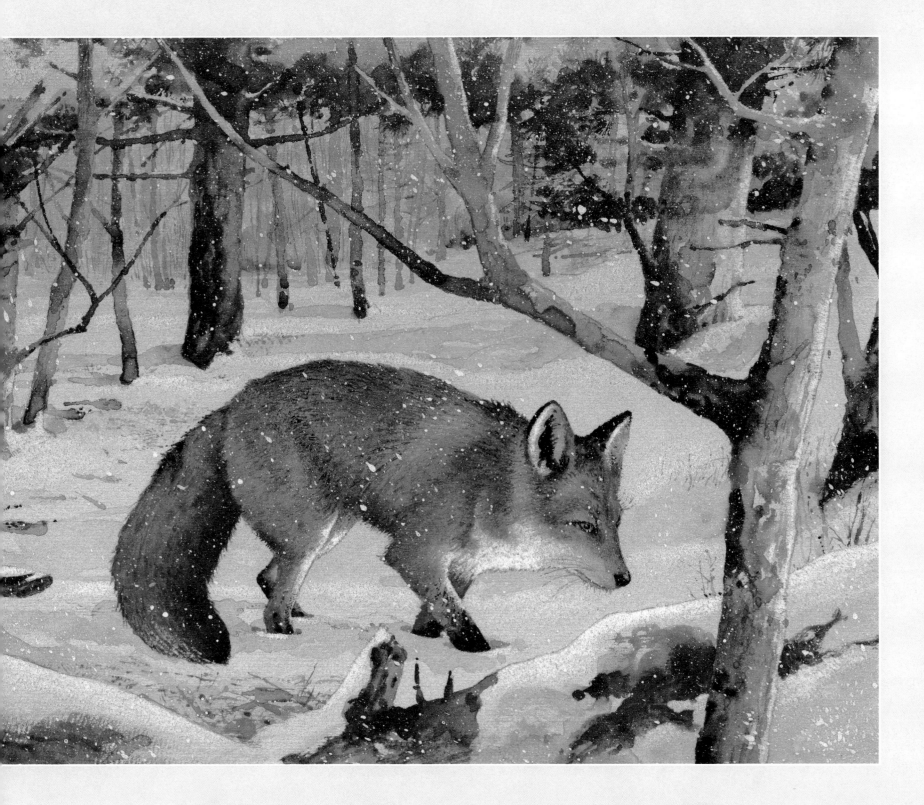

so he decides to follow the trail. The little fox is not looking for food, though. He is seeking out a woodchuck's burrow to take over for the bitter days ahead.

The coyote is not the only creature that the fox
must be aware of. Silhouetted in the moonlight,
a great tawny mountain lion is dangerously close. But

the powerful cat is preoccupied with the tracks of
another animal that he is stalking. The fox is safe for
now.

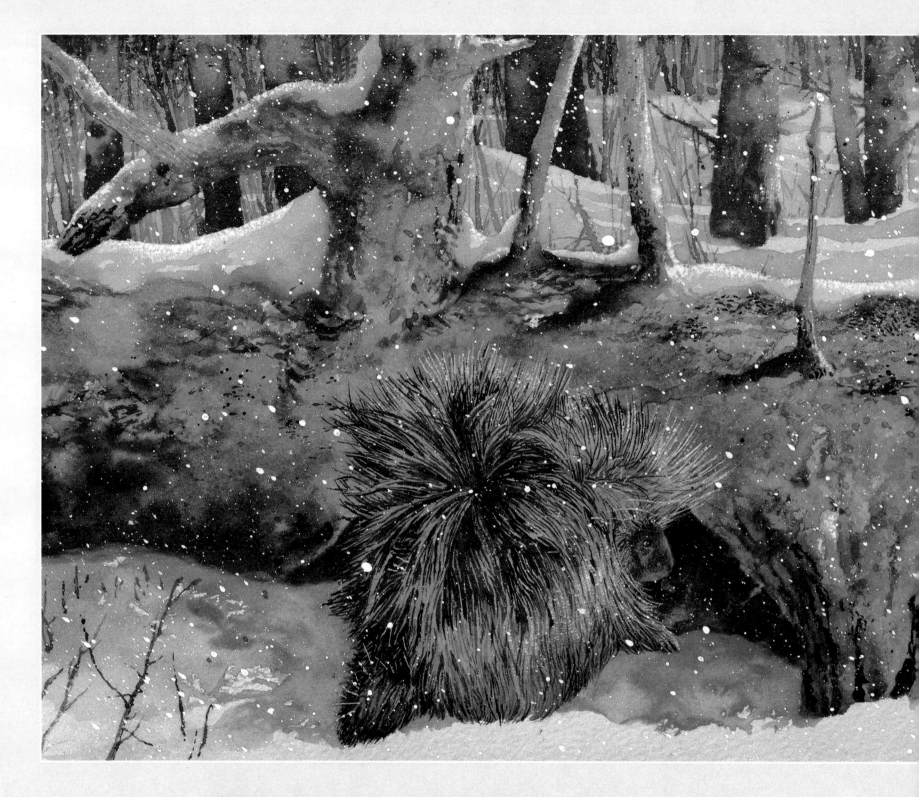

The mountain lion continues stalking his prey through the dense woodland. Once the cat is at a safe distance, a porcupine lumbers into the clearing

and up to a fallen fir tree. With quills loosely attached
to his skin, this small mammal will claim the hollow
arch in the tree as his den.

After removing the last bit of snow from the entrance
to his den, the porcupine crawls inside. He will
stay there until the snow stops falling. Not far away a
cottontail rabbit sits under a cedar tree munching on

twigs and leaves that have not been covered by the snow. Food is scarce and the rabbit has made a lucky find.

Once the cottontail has had his fill of food, he hops along the timberline on his way to the stream. As he starts down the embankment to the water, he senses danger and stands frozen. Suddenly he turns

and backtracks into the woodland. At the north fork
of the black stream, a hungry bobcat has located a
rodent under a fallen bough.

Busy beavers have built a dam at the south fork of the stream. In the middle of the artificial pool that has been created, a lone beaver has picked up the

scent of the bobcat. Hurriedly he swims up to a lodge
built of twigs, mud, and logs. In this lodge he will be
safe from the sleek cat.

Downstream from the beaver lodge, a long-tailed weasel, in his white winter coat, has also picked up the bobcat's scent. The frisky little weasel, knowing

he will not fare well against the cat, paddles across the
stream. He is headed for a familiar brushy area, where
he can easily escape from the predator.

Just around the bend from the brush where the long-tailed weasel has taken refuge, a curious raccoon shuffles out from behind a bush. This furry scavenger

with a bandit's face makes his way down to the stream,
where he will feed at the water's edge.

The raccoon soon discovers a large rainbow trout that has washed ashore. After filling himself with the tasty fish, he continues on his journey. Across the

water, near the mouth of the lake, a wet-furred river
otter slides down an icy bank into the swift current.

**W**hile the playful otter takes another run into the current, a mule deer trots down the embankment to the lake's rim. The graceful deer bends her slender neck and takes a drink of the cold water.

The mule deer turns away from the lake and makes her way toward a grove of pine trees. As dawn approaches, a soft light touches the tops of the lofty

pines. And high above in one of the trees, the great
horned owl will soon be asleep.

Across the lake and farther up the shore, the lights go on in the snow-covered cabin. In a few hours the sun will rise and chimney smoke from the breakfast hearth will signal the end of another North Country night.